W9-BZY-162

MILFORD ELEMENTARY
SCHOOL LIBRARY
MILFORD, NH

CELIA AND THE SWEET, SWEET WATER

by KATHERINE PATERSON

illustrated by VLADIMIR VAGIN

CLARION BOOKS
New York

MILFORD ELEMENTARY
SCHOOL LIBRARY
MILFORD, NH

Clarion Books
a Houghton Mifflin Company imprint
215 Park Avenue South, New York, NY 10003
Text copyright © 1998 by Minna Murra, Inc.
Illustrations copyright © 1998 by Vladimir Vagin

All rights reserved.
For information about permission to reproduce selections
from this book, write to Permissions, Houghton Mifflin Company,
215 Park Avenue South, New York, NY 10003.

Printed in Hong Kong

Library of Congress Cataloging-in-Publication Data
Paterson, Katherine.
Celia and the sweet, sweet water / by Katherine Paterson;
illustrated by Vladimir Vagin.—1st ed.
p. cm.
Summary: While journeying to find a remedy for her mother's illness,
Celia and her grumpy dog Brumble encounter strange
and threatening characters who have never known kindness.
ISBN 0-395-91324-1 (alk. paper)
[1. Mothers and daughters—Fiction.
2. Dogs—Fiction.   3. Kindness—Fiction.]
I. Vagin, Vladimir Vasilevich. 1937–   ill.   II. Title.
PZ7.P273Ce   1998   [E]—dc20   95-41632   CIP   AC

JDP   10 9 8 7 6 5 4 3 2 1

This story was written
for
Katherine Elizabeth Pierce
by
Nana-from-the-lake,
with love.

K.P.

to my daughter, Nastya

V.V.

Long ago in a tiny house deep in the countryside there lived a woman named Mara, her daughter, Celia, and a large, woolly, exceedingly grumpy dog named Brumble. Like most dogs who are members of a family, Brumble talked constantly. Sometimes Mara and Celia listened and sometimes they didn't.

Unlike Brumble, who was a complainer, Celia was nearly always happy, so it surprised her when, now and again, she would spy tears on her mother's lovely face.

Mara was remembering her childhood home and the husband of her youth and the terrible war that had robbed her of both. She never spoke to Celia of those sad times nor how, with only Brumble to protect them, she had fled with her infant daughter until she found at last a secluded cottage. Here they had been safe and comfortable for these ten years. When Celia caught her weeping, Mara simply brushed away her tears and played a lively tune on her wooden flute until both mother and daughter were cheerful again.

But Celia was not a spoiled or thoughtless child. She loved her mother very much, and so, one day when Mara fell ill, Celia set about to make her feel better. She brewed bark tea, rubbed her cold feet, and played soothing music on the wooden flute. Nothing helped. Mara tossed and turned, and her fever rose until she hardly seemed to know her daughter at all. Celia was nearly at her wits' end.

"What shall I do?" she cried.

"Fleabites and belly worms," grumbled Brumble. "I'll tell you what you can do. Quiet down and let an honest dog sleep."

Celia paid no attention to Brumble. She was used to his bad temper and worse manners. Besides, she was too worried about her mother to be bothered with Brumble's grumbling.

Just then her mother spoke. It was more like a person talking in her sleep than clear speech, but Celia heard her say something like: "If only I could drink once more the sweet, sweet water of my childhood, my life would be saved."

Now, Celia knew that Mara had been born many miles away in a village that Celia herself had never seen. Still, the brave girl determined at once to seek out the old village. She knew she must bring to her beloved mother the healing waters from its well.

Celia found a glass bottle with a cork stopper and tied it to her waist. She packed a little basket of bread and cheese because she knew the way would be long. She wrapped herself in Mara's cloak against the chilly spring air. And finally she stuck the wooden flute into her sash in case she needed music to cheer her along the path.

Then she leaned over and whispered in Mara's ear. "I'm going to fetch you the sweet, sweet water of your child-hood, Mother. There is food and drink on the table beside you. I'll be back soon."

Brumble opened one eye. "What's that you say? A child of your age wandering out alone? With no notion of the way?"

"It can't be helped," Celia said. "If I don't fetch the water, my mother will surely die."

"Oh, warm noses and cold feet." Brumble shuddered to his great furry paws. "I guess this means I'll have to go with you." Celia was grateful to have a companion on the road, even a grouchy one like Brumble.

It was midmorning when they set out. The sun was high, and the smell of new leaves and wildflowers filled the April air.

"What a wonderful day!" said Celia.

"Just wait," said Brumble. "It will change."

And sure enough, they had not gone very far before they came to the edge of a forest. There the trees grew so close together that even at noon the sun could hardly slip a ray of light between the tangled branches. Celia started to walk straight in amongst the trees. She didn't want Brumble to think she had lost her nerve.

Suddenly she heard a shriek so piercing that it seemed to tear the leaves from the tree limbs.

"What was that?" she cried, forgetting to act brave.

The big dog cocked his ear. "Alley cats and cockroaches. If it isn't the wild child of the woods."

If it's just another child, thought Celia, I don't care how wild he is. He's nothing to be afraid of.

Just then a creature came swinging out of the trees right at her, his hair shooting out in all directions and his mouth wide open in a terrible scream.

Celia took three deep breaths and swallowed hard. "Little boy," she managed to say quite politely, "don't you know it's rude not to say 'hello' to visitors? Brumble and I would like to be your friends. Now, if you'll stop that terrible noise and tell us what's the matter, we'll try to help you."

But the boy only snarled at her and scratched the air with his long, dirty fingernails.

"There, there," Celia said, trying to sound like her mother. "What you probably need is a good lunch. I just happen to have brought one, and if you'll mind your manners, we'll share it with you."

The wild child was astonished. No one had ever spoken to him so nicely before. The only other people he'd met in the woods took one look and ran as fast as they could in the opposite direction. The boy sat down on the ground and with a grimy hand patted the place beside him.

"There goes our lunch," grumped Brumble. And indeed it did. For Celia gave the cheese and almost all the bread to the wild child, who ate with great gusto and no manners at all.

"If you pass this way again," the wild child said, "be sure to stop and say 'hello.'" Celia promised that they would.

"Why bother?" grunted Brumble. "You've seen the last of our lunch."

When they came out of the forest on the other side, they were feeling a bit hungry. But Celia was really quite cheerful until she looked up and saw that directly ahead lay a great, green lake.

"Oh, rainy days and stickerburrs," grumbled Brumble. "I forgot the water."

"Listen," said Celia, for she had heard a strange sound. Someone was weeping, weeping, weeping, as though her heart might break.

"I also forgot about the wretched woman of the water." Brumble sighed. "I must be getting old."

As he spoke, Celia spied a little boat, and in the boat was a woman sobbing and crying so hard she never bothered to wipe her face.

Celia was a gentle-hearted child and felt pity for the woman. But she was also clever enough to realize that a boat would come in very handy.

"Dear lady," Celia said, "why are you so wretched?"

The woman's eyes opened wide in surprise. No one had ever bothered to ask her before. Usually the people she met just looked embarrassed and hurried around the lake on foot.

"I'm cold and lonely," she said. "I haven't a friend in the world."

"Why," said Celia, "I have just what you need, a nice warm cloak and two pleasant"—here she gave Brumble a hard look—"traveling companions who will cross the lake with you in your lovely little boat and tell you exciting stories as we go."

"Bee stings and billy goats," Brumble humphed. But he was glad to jump aboard and save his paws that long way round on the rocky shore.

The woman was no longer wretched when she let them off on the farther side. She was wrapped in Mara's warm cloak and wore a friendly smile. "Thank you," she called. "Be sure to ride with me again when you return."

"We'd be glad to," said Celia. For once Brumble did not grumble.

The stone-strewn beach where they landed ended at a line of boulders. Celia's heart sank, for towering above the huge rocks was a mountain.

"*Hot* noses and *frozen* feet," grouched Brumble. "I forgot about the mountain."

"Who dares trespass on my shore?" a furious voice called out.

Celia looked up and there on the side of the mountain was the largest, angriest man she had ever seen. He was swinging a huge ax as though he meant to hurl it right at her.

"My goodness, but you're angry," she said, and her voice only shook a little.

"I also forgot the mad man of the mountain," Brumble murmured under his breath.

"Do you know what soothes me when I am out of sorts?" Celia asked the man, growing braver with every word. "Music. Would you like me to play for you?"

Without waiting for an answer, she took the flute from her sash and began to play.

By the water, music sounds even lovelier than it does in a closed room, and the angry man cocked his head to listen. Soon he let the ax drop to his side. Finally he sat down on the rocks, his face free of fury for the first time in many years.

When Celia stopped playing, he looked so sad that she climbed up the boulders and handed him the flute. "Here," she said. "It's for you. So that you'll be able to make music whenever you wish."

"Can't you stay and teach me how to play?" the man asked.

"I can for a little while," Celia said. "But I am in a terrible hurry. I must draw some water from the well in the village on the other side of this mountain and take it home to save my mother's life."

"Then I will carry you across the mountain," the man said, "and you can teach me as we go."

Brumble struggled up the boulders and came padding up all in a pant, but the man made no effort to hoist him to his shoulder. "Ear mites and mangy fur," rumbled Brumble. "It's a dog's life."

Going up the mountain, Celia played a song that was merry enough to make the man laugh out loud. When they reached the top, she showed him how to blow and where to put his fingers, and going down she clung to his hair so that he could practice.

When the man had gently put Celia on her feet, he played a little tune to prove what a good teacher she was. "Call out when you return," he said, "and I'll give you a ride over the mountain once more."

Celia gladly promised to do so, but Brumble only growled under his breath.

When she realized that the village they had sought so long was just over the next hill, Celia forgot her hunger and cold and weariness, and she ran ahead. She only had eyes for the well in the middle of the square. "There it is, Brumble," she cried. "There's the well with the sweet, sweet water of my mother's childhood."

Her cry echoed in the empty street. Grass grew between the cobblestones. From the crumbling walls of the houses

and the balding roofs, Celia could tell that the village had long been deserted.

"Never mind," she said as bravely as ever. "All we came for was a little bottle of water. There's sure to be some water left in the well." She leaned over the edge and peered down. She could see nothing but blackness.

Brumble picked up a pebble in his mouth and tossed it over the edge. They listened until finally, far below, they heard a faint *plink*.

"Hooray!" cried Celia. "There's water!"

"Failure and frustration," grumbled Brumble. "Water, but no bucket to draw it up."

Indeed, when Celia looked, she realized that someone had stolen the bucket, leaving only the frayed rope behind. Without a word she clambered up on the edge of the well and tied the end of the old rope around her waist. "Now, Brumble," she said, "you must let me down gently. When I call up to you, hold the crank perfectly still, give me time to fill my bottle, and then wind me slowly back to the top."

Brumble was not pleased with this plan. What if the crank should slip? What if the rope should break? But however fluttery Celia felt inside, outside she was firm as iron. She had come too far to let anything stop her now.

Headfirst she went—down, down into the dark depths

of the well. She could not see the water, but in her mind's eye she could see her mother's beautiful face, and it gave her courage. At last she felt the water's coolness on her outstretched hand.

"Stop!" she called up to Brumble, who held his great paw steady on the crank while she filled the bottle and stoppered it securely. "I have it!" she cried. "Bring me up!"

Paw over paw, Brumble wound the rusty crank, not daring to breathe until his precious burden was safely on solid ground.

"There!" said Celia. "That wasn't hard, now, was it?"

"Tremblings and palpitations," grunted Brumble. "I am too old for adventuring." With his rough, red tongue, he washed her dirty face.

The trip home was far speedier than the earlier journey. The man (no longer mad) carried Celia back over the mountain and played a lovely tune for her while they waited for poor, panting Brumble to catch up with them. The woman (no longer wretched) rowed them across the lake and wished them all kinds of good fortune. And the child (no longer quite as wild) swung through the trees crying "Hello! Hello! Hellooooo!" making Celia laugh, the birds squawk, and Brumble grumble.

When they saw their own dear house, Celia broke into a run. "We're home," she cried, snatching the precious bottle from her waist. "Take heart, Mother, I'm back with the sweet, sweet water of your childhood!"

"Care and caution," muttered Brumble. "A journey isn't done until it's over."

And he was right, for in her haste, Celia tripped on the stairs. The bottle flew out of her hand and was dashed to pieces against the stone foundation of the cottage.

The priceless water splashed against the stones and dribbled down onto the ground.

Celia could not bear to watch. She ran into the house and flung herself on her mother's body. It was still as death.

"Oh, Mother, I've failed you!" Celia cried out. "How could I be so careless? How could I be so stupid?"

Poor Celia felt as wild as the child, as angry as the man and, oh, my friends, far more wretched than the woman. She wept as though her heart had shattered into a thousand shards, her tears cascading like a waterfall down her cheeks and splashing onto her mother's lifeless face.

Just then her mother's pale lips parted. With the tip of her tongue she took a tiny taste of the tears that were flowing down upon her. Slowly, she smiled.

"Such sweet water," she murmured, opening her eyes. "It is the same sweet, sweet water that I remember from my childhood. And you, my dearest Celia, have brought it home to me."

Through all the years of their long lives, Mara and Celia knew a joy that many people never know—indeed, that neither of them had known before the day when they discovered that you cannot truly share another's happiness unless you share her tears.

As for Brumble, he got older and older and was never more pleased than when he had something to grumble about.